FIVE IN WAITING

Conversations of Faith in the E.R.

JIM GARFINKEL

Five in Waiting: Conversations of Faith in the E.R.
Copyright 2025 by Jim Garfinkel

Illustrations by Kacey Garfinkel, Kacey Rey's Art

Paperback ISBN 978-1-957497-57-0

Published in the United States of America

CONTENTS

ACKNOWLEDGMENTS

As Jesus taught us to start our prayers by praising and worshiping God, I do so here. If not for him, this effort that is resting in your hands would not be possible. It is in his hands that I place this story and pray he uses it to further his kingdom.

Buckets of thanks must be poured out upon my wife, Katie, and my two daughters, Kacey and Jessie. They were instrumental in their support and encouragement. When I wanted to go over the top with all aspects of this story, they pulled me back. When I despaired and wanted to quit, they propped me up. (They also patiently put up with a not-pleasant human being at those times).

Tom Reed, a fellow drama guy, church elder, friend, and an amazing copy editor, must be acknowledged for all the time he gave to punctuation, grammar, and word selection before this was sent to the publishing copy editors, whom I also thank. Pastor Mark Johnson, the lead pastor at Grace Fellowship Church in Jackson, California, also deserves my thanks and acknowledgment. It was his idea, many years ago, that led to this fictional biblical story of apologetics and theology so that he could present his sermon series in a creative way.

Finally, to you who read and perhaps utilize these words
to further your Christian walk or to assist others in theirs,
thank you, and may God lead you further into his kingdom.

INTRODUCTION

I guess this introduction is more of an explanation of the who, what, and why of what follows on the next pages. I'm sort of a church drama guy. Not the guy that revels in stirring up issues within the church congregation, but one who writes scripts for skits, plays, and videos for our church. Way back in 2007, the pastor of the church we were attending, Pastor Mark Johnson (whom I thank for his vision of this project), asked me if I would write a series of skits about some of the attributes of Jesus Christ for an upcoming series of sermons he was preparing. Attributes such as Jesus the suffering servant, Jesus the compassionate Savior, and Jesus the Messiah and king were on the list.

Armed with the pastor's vision and uncertain if I had it in me to write these vignettes (I tend to use humor rather than emotion-charged dialogue when trying to make a point through my drama scripts), I went to my knees. I prayed. I studied. I prayed some more. Eventually, the Holy Spirit planted the idea of the series of skits I titled "Five in Waiting." The idea was to have the same actors in the same setting for each skit. Each character would be utilized, hopefully clearly, to present an attribute of Jesus in some way that the pastor could use in his sermons to accentuate his points.

But where would a group of five people from different walks of life, with different worldviews, gather together?

Again, with a push from the Holy Spirit, I landed on the idea of a hospital waiting room, an area where emotions, pain, relief, fear, and empathy—or lack of it—are on full display. The skits seemed to write themselves, as did many of my scripts. Pastor Mark read and approved them with nary a correction or suggestion, which means he either didn't really read them, or he trusted me, or it was actually what he was looking for. I prefer to believe in the last choice, as it supports the presence of miracles.

Fast forward to 2024. I started translating the scripts into this novella form in 2012, and then, for some reason, the Holy Spirit said, "Wait." So, I walked away. My daughters asked me several times if I would ever finish it. I never really answered them until I placed the first three chapters in front of them and asked them to let me know, after they read it, if I should finish it. When I wrote this introduction, they did not tell me a thing because they hadn't read it. However, my wife did and has given me some valuable developmental editor-type insights. Her response encouraged me to finish it, to which the Holy Spirit apparently agreed and, thankfully, assisted.

At the end of each chapter are some Bible verses that apply to the theme of that chapter, and I hope you will explore them and take them to heart. At the end of the story, I am including the original scripts that inspired this effort and were well received by all involved in their production. If any pastor or drama person wishes to use them, please do. You have my permission. You are welcome to change some things in them so they can better fit your church's personality. You owe me no fees or royalties. I only ask that you let me know how you used them and how it all went. You can reach me through my website in this world, www.atfarmveterinaryservices.com. (Yes, after I finish doing drama stuff, I pull on a pair of coveralls, and I step into the other ministry God has placed me: an equine veterinarian.)

CHAPTER ONE

MATTHEW

This moment could have happened at any time. Today, yesterday, or any day or night of the week. Still, God works in amazing ways, and he arranged for it all to happen last Christmas Eve. *Christmas Eve.* Just mention the night, and images begin forming in your mind. Joy and peace. Calm and quiet. Family and friends. Snow and crackling fireplaces. Smells of scented candles, Christmas trees, and baked sweets. Perhaps the sounds of Christmas stimulate your thoughts of Christmas Eve. The singing of carols, the laughter, and the tinkling of ornaments. Or maybe you smile inwardly when you recall the excitement in a child's eyes as they anticipate the opening of gifts. Or do you wonder in awe at what it would have been like ... if you only could have been there ... that first Christmas Eve, when our Savior was born, to witness that miracle?

As long as I can remember, Christmas Eve has had that effect on me. I was the child who was boiling over, anticipating the arrival of my gifts. The family tradition was to open the "out-of-town relatives" gifts on Christmas Eve. Aunt Flossy always sent a brand-new crisp five-dollar bill. Grandma Hickle always sent an ornament, which we were to put away until we were grown-ups and had our own tree (which at the time seemed rather useless, but for which I am now extremely thankful). Later on, in my college years, Christmas Eve became a time to enjoy with family and to take a much-needed sabbatical from school.

Then I found the girl of my dreams, and Christmas Eve became even more alive. It was Joy who made my world brighter and happier. New Christmas Eve traditions were started, and I looked forward to the night more than I did as a wide-eyed, innocent child. We'd trade off years; one Christmas, we would visit Joy's family, the next, my family, and then one to ourselves.

And then our little girl arrived. It was not until she was born that I truly stopped and saw the wonder of Christmas, the wonder of God. The incredible gift of a child. Not just our little girl, but the gift of that infant born in the stable on that beautiful silent night. Joy and I took even more notice and began to seek him. *Jesus. The Christ.* The only begotten Son of God. The Savior of mankind who was promised and hinted at throughout the entire Bible. Soon, all the wonders of Christmas Eve were a heightened symphony to me.

Yes, all the images and wonders of Christmas Eve engulfed me every year of my life. Except for two.

Those two Christmas Eves were the ones you read about in magazines or watch people cry about while being interviewed during a television talk show. They were the first two Christmas Eves I spent as an adult without my wife and daughter. *Alone.* Oh, sure, friends and family would invite me over or come to visit. My pastor and church friends would pray with me and assure me my wife and daughter were with Jesus in a place so wonderful that we couldn't even begin to contemplate it. But Christmas Eve had lost its joy, its wonder, its meaning.

I never really knew what a crisis of faith was until that dark time in my life. It's when all those questions not meant for us to understand come streaming to the forefront, when there can be anger at God for taking away, for no good reason you can see, ones you loved so dearly. I had a seething hatred of that drug-addicted fool who crashed into their car that awful summer night. That was how I spent Christmas Eve for two years straight—me yelling at God and him listening and taking it. By doing so, he was comforting me without me realizing it. Then, when the third Christmas Eve without Joy and little Rae arrived, I received an amazing gift. For the first time in my life, I decided to flip the mattress. That frustrating chore yielded a treasure I never knew existed: Joy's diary. I shook and cried as I read it. In her words, I found that I had never really lost the faith we shared together. I read the Bible verses she had quoted. I reminisced with her in my mind about so many things, and I prayed. I prayed with fervor and meaning. Then, somewhere deep inside me, a flame began to warm me. Christmas Eve was back but altered.

That was ten years ago. All the wonders that make Christmas Eve what it is remain, but my feelings of excitement now come from a different source. This last Christmas Eve is a great example. You see, in my despondency after the loss of my family, I sold my business and hibernated. Buried in my grief and descending deeper and deeper into my personal vortex, I found work as a security guard at our local hospital. I requested the night shift, as I figured I wouldn't have to interact with many people, and I would be able to sleep throughout the day, thereby avoiding any human contact whatsoever. After all, people would either be admitted to a bed and fall asleep or be absorbed in their own misfortune while waiting for hours upon hours in the emergency room.

However, after I read Joy's diary, the people in the waiting room or lying in their beds waiting to be healed suddenly became more than just unfortunate people. They became souls. Souls that could be torn apart, as I had been. Souls that might be confused and scared as they waited to hear the medical verdict on themselves or a loved one. I began to squeeze out of my self-inflicted internal exile and talk to them. I let my faith guide me, and over the years, I learned things I never knew. I found contentment in comforting others at a time of need, and I found my faith in God abound.

Then came last Christmas Eve. I had spoken about Jesus with hundreds, maybe even thousands, of patrons at the hospital over the years. There were the naysayers, the polite listeners, the believers, the seekers, and the virulent anti-religious fanatics. But never had the four gospels been so forced into conversation than on this particular Christmas Eve, which gave me no other option but to explain, interpret, and defend them. For the first time in my life, I wished I had paid more attention in Sunday School as a kid. It even made me feel as if I wasn't paying enough attention to the Sunday morning messages at worship services as an adult!

The evening started innocently enough. It was near the end of my shift, and, per my regular routine, I took that time to head down to the hospital's emergency room waiting area to eat and to see if I could comfort a soul or two while I was down there. One benefit of being a security guard at this hospital was the freedom of location. I could walk the halls, sit at a desk waiting for a call, or hang out in the waiting room for as long as I wanted. An even better perk was that Stella, the check-in manager, made the best coffee for the patrons down there. The liquid in the staff room resembled hot water with a black crayon dipped in it, and the vending machine that advertised great coffee spit out some liquid substance that NASA probably couldn't even identify. As I entered the room, I noticed a handful of people sitting around the waiting area, trying to act as if they were calm and comfortable. There was a young lady sitting in a wheelchair with an intravenous drip running into her arm. She was wrapped in a terry cloth robe and had a scarf around her head. The look of a cancer patient is one we all know, and I breathed a short, silent prayer for her.

To her right were a father and his teenage daughter. He was sporting a lot of Las Vegas Raiders' attire but didn't look like one of the face-painted maniacs whose goal in life was to be seen by millions on Sunday telecasts. While he banged away on his laptop, apparently trying to make a living, I quickly observed his daughter. She was actually studying a world history textbook. Dressed in a nondescript manner, she seemed to have an air of confidence about herself. She occasionally glanced at her father's laptop as if to make sure he was still working and not playing the latest Madden video game. They exchanged knowing family looks with each other, and if someone pressed me to decide, based on my first impression, which of the two was the more mature, I'd have been tempted to choose the teenager.

The person who stood out, though, was the long-haired lady in the lotus position. Having relocated several cushions from a few of the waiting room's couches and chairs, she was positioned, in her own way, comfortably on the floor. In front of her, she had a handful of lovely colored crystals, which she occasionally shuffled around as if she were playing three-card monte with some invisible friend. She wore a tie-dye dress, a set of unmatched colorful stockings, and, to finish off her look, a pair of popular brand-name high-top basketball shoes. I was glad to see she was not one of the emergency room doctors.

As I approached the coffee carafe, I thought I'd break the ice with everyone by offering up a cup of Stella's caffeinated wonder to anyone interested. "Anyone up for a cup?" While the others shook their heads politely, Raiders Dad spoke up as he glanced at his watch.

"Ya know what? Yeah, I could use another boost. Looks like we're in for a long night. Might as well be wired for it."

"That's life in the E.R. waiting room," I sympathized. After all, I had spent countless hours sitting in the very chair he now occupied, praying for my wife and daughter. I remember spending hours wondering if the interior decorator chose the mauve and purple color scheme to soothe the patron's anxiety or to attempt to encourage it. "How long have you been here?"

"About an hour," he replied.

"Two hours," his daughter corrected playfully yet politely.

"Or two hours," he parroted as he threw a look at his girl. "They just took my wife to radiology, and they told me to expect ..." His words hung in the air, as did his jaw, as he stared over my shoulder in what can only be described as disbelief. I turned and followed his gaze to the double doors that led to the emergency room medical floor, where a young man had just stumbled out. He looked to be in his early twenties, had a bandage on his head, a fresh cast on his left arm, and a backpack slung over his right shoulder. He appeared to be not just bruised and battered but inebriated as well. My first impression was that he was on the verge of tears, but when he looked up and became aware of several pairs of eyes on him, his demeanor became more defensive and insolent. His gaze fell on me.

I held up the coffee pot. "Coffee's on me, son. Need a cup?"

"No, I don't need a cup of coffee," he shot back. "And I don't appreciate you cleverly pointing out that I've had a couple of Christmas Eve celebratory egg-nogs!" Noticing the sideways glances of the others in the room, he spread his arms as wide as his cast allowed him to and yelled, "Yes! I've been out drinking! Thank you very much!" and then crashed down into a chair. Even our little crystal gazer on the floor flinched, though she pretended to be uninterested and deep in meditation.

I tried to defuse his explosiveness. "Sorry, son. I was only offering, not judging."

"And I'm not your son!" he salvoed. "My name's Matt. Not Son, or Sonny, or Son of a... Look, I can tell you all think I'm hammered right now, and a few hours ago, you'd have been right. But right now, I'm as sober as a judge."

The sound of his pause was disconcerting. As he spoke again, my discomfort gave way to concern. I felt as if I should pity him, but instead, I sensed a need to listen to him and somehow help. "Seeing two of your best friends die, and one on life support, in just a matter of a few hours? Well, that has a way of sobering you up really quick."

I glanced back at the Raiders fan and noticed he had returned to adroitly pounding on his laptop. A quick scan also revealed, for the first time, sitting off in a corner by herself, a rather nondescript lady, watching the entire scene.

As Matt slouched onto a couch, I delivered the coffee to the Raiders guy and went back to scoop up my cafeteria slop. Then I headed to the seat nearest Matt. "Look, I'm sorry, Matt. About your friends and all. I wasn't trying to poke fun at you or even suggest you were drunk. I really was just offering you a cup of coffee. I had just finished offering one to everyone else when you came in." Out of the corner of my eye, I caught the daughter of the Raiders fan nodding her head in support. My mind flashed a little note to itself:. *You have a friend in this room tonight.* "Ya know, I work here every night except Sundays, and well, I never really know what everyone's story is. So, as odd and, maybe, as nosey as it may sound, I come in here on my lunch hour or at the end of my shift to see if I can make the wait in this place a little easier on people. I've found that sometimes just talking helps pass the time. My mom always said it can help folks to have someone, anyone, listen to whatever is running through their minds."

Matt's sarcasm reflected his pain. "Oh, I see. You're a rent-a-cop first and a shrink second. That's lovely. Maybe you should try your hand at stand-up comedy. That might help the time pass a little faster."

Hoping to defuse his vitriol, I smiled and said, "I don't have any comic material. I'm not a shrink. And I'm not rented. The hospital sorta owns me."

He wasn't amused. "Well, thanks. It's a great comfort knowing the hospital that has my friend's life in its hands made such a pristine hire for a security guard. Where did you get your crime-fighting education, a trailer park?"

A momentary flashback when I received my MBA filled my memory and almost made me blurt out a caustic response. But somewhere, somehow, I heard these words leave my mouth: "Something like that." He stared at me, and I suddenly realized that he was indeed communicating, not just tossing me aside, so I let the words flow. "Listen, Matt. Instead of looking for someone to vent on, maybe you should be thanking God that you're in this room, and"—I motioned to the double door leading to triage—"not in any of the ones back there anymore."

His eyes went wide, and I thought I saw a flash of confusion, which morphed into anger. "Thank?!" The color in his face seemed to suggest that there were over one hundred shades of red in the color spectrum. "Look, Paul Blart, I'd rather be ... I'd trade places with Freddie back there in a heartbeat. He didn't even want to go with us tonight! I'm the one that talked him into it!" Matt quieted, and the red colors defused to blue as shame and sorrow seeped through. "He just got married a few months ago. His wife was working overtime tonight, and I told him we'd have him home in time to meet her at the door under the mistletoe. I ought to be the one back there, not him."

The others in the room were not making any pretenses. They were paying attention. The lady undergoing chemo had lowered the magazine she was reading. Raiders fan was watching passively, and his daughter was encouraging me with soulful eyes. The 1960s' leftover in the lotus position was not as active in rearranging her crystals, a sure sign she was listening. And the lady in the corner? Well, she seemed to have sharpened her attentiveness. She appeared genuinely interested in the exchange.

"I know exactly what you mean," I said solemnly, for I meant it. "I screamed the same thing numerous times when my wife and daughter died. It took me a long time to realize this, but I can guarantee you that there are a lot of people, while grieving the loss of your two friends and praying for Freddie to recover, are very happy that you're alright."

He waved me off. "Naw. No one. Really."

Before I knew it, the words came out of my mouth. "I actually know someone who does." Matt's look of surprise was immediately replaced with one of disgust when I said, "Jesus is."

With an amazing dramatic flair, Matt flung his arms up in the air and shouted, "Oh, great! A rent-a-cop, a shrink, and now a religious Bible thumper! You wanna get into it now, Jesus freak? 'Cause I will. I'm a graduate student at U.C. Berkeley. I've taken classes on"—he began to tick off on his fingers—"world religions, philosophy, astrology, anthropology, evolution, as well as a plethora of other subjects. So, believe me when I say you don't want to even start trying to comfort me with religion. I don't need the crutch."

"I'm not talking about religion, Matt." I waited until he looked at me again to see if that registered. If nothing else, it caught him a little off guard. "I'm talking about Jesus. A real person and about real Christianity." He stared at me but said nothing. I was about to push on when a sweet, weak voice chimed in.

"Sorry to interrupt, Mister...?" The cancer patient hung on the "Mister" as one does when trying to get a name.

I obliged. "Michael."

"Michael." Her voice seemed to have a resonance to it, even in its frailty. "But Christianity *is* a religion. At least the last time I looked, it was."

The statement that I baited Matt with had encouraged another fish to nibble. Maybe more, judging from the stares I was getting from all around the room. "Not really. You see, religion is when people try to find their way to God. But Christianity is different. It's about God coming directly to people through Jesus Christ and allowing every person to develop a personal relationship with God."

As many a Raiders fan can, the silver-and-black-clad guy spoke up. Which meant that the night was looking to get interesting. "Same difference," he said. "It's double-speak like that that gets folks all confused and crazy. Next thing you know, they're throwing up their hands in church, singing obnoxiously loud, and making everyone else uncomfortable!"

"Excuse me?!" His daughter looked at him incredulously. Yep, this was definitely shaping up to be a really interesting night. "Okay, Dad," she said. Rather sarcastically, I might add. Pointing directly into his face as she challenged him. "Try to guess who I am now." She leaned forward on the couch, her elbows resting on her knees, and looked straight ahead. She began to clench a fist. Her mock excitement rising, she bounced in her chair as she blurted out, "Go ... go ... GO! YES!" She then proceeded to jump up in the air, both arms extended above her head, jumping up and down, yelling, "Touchdown,

Raaaaaiders!" She did a funky celebration dance and added, "Oh yeah. Oh yeah. The silver and black attack is back!"

While everyone in the room stifled their smiles—even Matt—her father just stared at her for a beat before trying to mount his defense. "That's different. That's ... you know ... sports! It's, umm, exciting spur-of-the-moment stuff," he stammered.

"Oh, I see," his daughter continued professorially. I was really beginning to like this kid. "So, people in a church, while having an exciting, strong, meaningful moment with God, the Creator of the universe, *their* Creator, while having a moment of joy that causes them to raise their hands in worship, you think *that's* 'crazy' behavior? You *actually* think that your conduct watching a sports moment is more appropriate than if that same type of enthusiasm is used to show someone's joy in worshiping God?"

"Well, when the Raiders score, it is a small miracle." The lotus-positioned lady smiled. She must have been a Chargers fan.

Matt decided to re-enter the fray. "Yeah, well, when it comes to religion, been there, done that. I was raised in the Jewish faith, and after I matured and became independent, I tried several others. I've been dunked, sprinkled, splashed, sprayed, doused, hosed down; you name it. And where did it get me? An emergency room with two dead friends and one barely alive."

"And you, very much alive," said the cancer patient

honestly.

I felt the moment was right, so I faced Matt. "And thank God for that, Matt. You have a second chance. All you're going through tonight: the fear, the frustration, the loss, and the grief—it need not be in vain. I know you've heard it before, but it's true. Christ came to save you. He wants a relationship with you, and he wants to help you be the person you're created to be."

"Christ?" Matt spit his name out in a display of disbelief. "My professor for World Religions said that there is no proof that Jesus was anything more than a great teacher. That what we call the Old Testament is a myth. Jesus doesn't even make it to prophet status. As for him being the Messiah? My father, a Jew, spoke of a messianic age, not an individual Messiah. In fact, he showed me that not even half of the prophecies were fulfilled by Jesus. Sorry to burst your holy bubble, but Jesus doesn't fit the bill to be the Christ." As he finished, his conviction seemed to be laced with sadness. I was about to press a little more when the lotus lady, glaring at me with a devilish grin, seized her opportunity.

"Ah, prophecies! What a great place to begin the search. Go ahead, Michael. What about the prophecies of the Bible? Please explain how you Christians make the square peg of Jesus fit into the round hole of prophecy?"

Her challenge was followed by an almost instantaneous head-turning as all in the room looked at me either expectantly, curiously, or defiantly. I started with the easy stuff in the book of Isaiah and moved on from there.

I could have gone on for hours, but after about 15 minutes, I decided to rest my case. After all, Jesus' life and death do more than fulfill the prophecies. He fulfills God's promise to us all. Proclaiming the good news is more than just debating prophecy and scripture.

But, tell you what. Instead of repeating all I said about it that night in the waiting room, here are some things to look at in the Gospel of Matthew. Trust me, there's no better way to understand and learn the truth than to dive into the Bible yourself. Try praying before you start for God to help you see and understand his meaning. Stop occasionally and pray a few words while you're reading as well. God wants you to understand and believe his Word. Then come on back, and I'll tell you what transpired next on that amazing Christmas Eve in that waiting room.

JESUS IS THE CHRIST, THE MESSIAH

Matthew 1:23:
The virgin birth prophesied in Isaiah 7:14
Matthew 2:5-6:
Born in Bethlehem prophesied in Micah 5:2
Matthew 21:4:
Triumphant entry into Jerusalem referencing

Zechariah 9:9
Matthew 26:53-54:
*Betrayal by Judas referencing Zechariah
11:12*

Note that Matthew, in many verses, states, "This was to fulfill what was spoken by the prophet." By connecting Jesus' life events to the Old Testament prophecies, Matthew presents a very strong case to his readers that Jesus is the Messiah.

QUESTIONS TO THINK ABOUT AND DISCUSS

1.   Why do you think the author chose Christmas Eve for the timing of this story? (Hint: While Christmas celebrates the birth of Jesus, what do the Old Testament scriptures say will be shown in his character and life?- Isaiah 9-)

2.   List three of the responses presented to Matt by Michael. Have you ever encountered any of these points in a discussion? What else could Michael have said to Matt at this point in support of the Christian faith?

3.   Matt makes the accusation that Jesus was merely a good teacher, not the Messiah. Other than the fulfillment of prophecy, how else might one respond to such a remark?

4.   What are two Old Testament scriptures (not listed above) that either point to the coming Messiah or to God's ultimate plan of salvation for mankind?

CHAPTER TWO

MARGARET

The sky outside of the west windows was turning a deep purple as I finished my dissertation on prophecy fulfillment. I finished with the non-debatable point of mathematics. "So, there you have it. The probabilities of the prophecies in the Old Testament being fulfilled by one man, Jesus, are astounding, if not insurmountable. One of the main reasons that many of the Jews of that time felt that Jesus did not fulfill many prophecies is because the prophecies could not be confirmed to be fulfilled until after Christ's death, resurrection, and ascension." The broad smile on Raiders fan's daughter warmed my heart and confirmed that the information I presented was worthwhile. I prayed a quick, silent prayer asking God to keep me focused on his wants and apologizing to him if I slipped up anywhere without catching it. The fluorescent lights seemed to brighten a bit overhead as I sipped my coffee. It tasted better than it ever had before.

"Prophecies ..." The sweet voice of our cancer patient trailed off as she winced in pain. She leaned forward in her wheelchair as the intravenous line followed her arm to her abdomen, which she pressed to relieve the discomfort. "Prophecies are one thing. Fairness is another."

This seemed like an odd transition, but her expression indicated that her concerns on this matter were deep and unanswered. "I don't follow you," I said with interest.

She spoke with an anguish that did not come from her physical pain. "I'm a single mother of two. I'm here because of a reaction I'm having to a chemo treatment I had today. I've been getting ..." She trailed off as another wave of pain riddled her weakened body. "So, my question is..." she spoke as she raised her head. Her liquid brown eyes were full of confusion and concern. At that moment, it was as if only three of us were in the room—she, I, and Jesus. "My question is, *why me*?" She said it with no trace of animosity or resentment. Just an honest disbelief of her circumstances. "I mean. I can deal with my pain to a point. I can suffer through it. I get some relief from the pain medications. But why would God have my children suffer, too? My parents are gone, and I was an only child." She faltered. "I have no one to care for my kids. I mean, I'm looking. I'm asking friends. I'm desperately looking for someone to love and care for them when I die." She hung her head in surrender. "The pain I feel for my girls is worse than any physical pain from the cancer," she finished.

I heard the Raiders fan quietly say to no one in particular, "And there it is. The age-old question. Why do bad things happen to good people?" He spoke quietly, yet everyone seemed to hear it. I could feel them all begin to nod slowly.

My eyes had not wandered from our sweet chemo patient. My heart was full, yet my mind was numb. *Say something!* I thought. *Anything!* Her head rose, and her brown eyes glistened with moisture as they met mine. I heard my voice from far away. "May I pray for you and your girls?" Her eyes steadied as the corners of her mouth tilted ever so slightly upward, and she nodded. As she quickly looked away, I approached her and kneeled beside her, taking care not to bump her wheelchair or I.V. stand. "I'm sorry," I stammered, "I didn't ask your name yet."

"Margaret," she replied. "Margaret Marks." She actually held out her hand for me to shake as an introduction.

As she did so, I clasped both my hands onto hers and prayed in earnest. I did not look to see if anyone else had bowed their heads with us, but I was confident that the Raiders fan's daughter would. "Father God, we lift up Margaret to you today. We ask that you place your healing hand upon her. And if it is your will, remove the cancer that she has bravely been fighting. Help the doctors to find the correct treatments and ease her pain—the pain from the cancer, the pain in her life, and the pain of worry and concern she has for her children. I pray that you ease her suffering, Lord. Because you, Jesus, the Son that has suffered the most, can understand her pain and suffering. We know you can provide her with the utmost comfort at this time. Lord Jesus, we know that your greatest time of suffering was also your greatest service to us. We ask you to be with Margaret and her children. Comfort them. Look over them. We ask that you give her and her children the strength and courage they will need in the days ahead, that you will comfort them in their times of sorrow and fear. Finally, Lord, we pray that if it is necessary, you raise up good, loving people who Margaret can entrust her children to. That it will be a loving and safe home for them to grow up in. I pray all this in the name of our precious Savior, Jesus Christ. Amen."

"Thank you," she whispered.

I nodded weakly, as I felt somewhat spent. As I pivoted to return to my seat, the room seemed to whirl in a dizzying array of colors as I heard her ask in the strongest voice I had heard from her that evening, "Michael? I noticed, when you were praying that you said Jesus had suffered the most. I'm sure the pain on the cross was awful, but others were crucified back then as well. How was his suffering any worse than theirs? Or any more painful than others who were beaten and tortured at the hands of the Romans?"

"Because he suffered the sufferings of *all* of us." It was the Raiders fan's daughter. Everyone in the room turned to look at her, their expressions filled with surprise, especially her father's. As she quickly surveyed the faces of all in the room, her eyes latched onto her father's. "What?"

I tried to rescue her. "Wow. That's right." I tried to sound somewhat playful. "I know they don't teach that in our public school systems, so where ..."

Her father waved it off with his hand as he intoned, "Her mother takes her to church."

"And you don't go with them." I wasn't asking it as a question. My tone indicated it was more of a statement than a question. While he looked away, his daughter took the opportunity to interject her thoughts on the matter.

"Someday he will. He doesn't know it yet, but he will." As she looked at him, she continued. "The whole church is praying for him." The look of mock terror on his face brought chuckles all around, even to the lotus lady. I guess his daughter decided teasing him again would be a good bonding tactic, because she added, "Right now, he worships at the altar of the Las Vegas Raiders."

"Just win, baby!" He smiled broadly as he looked at me. "Raiders 3:16."

Matthew chimed in. "Not sure even prayer will help that team." I gave some quick thanks to God that Matt was at least listening to the conversations.

I decided it was better to return to Margaret before the ball began rolling down the wrong path. "She's right, you know, Margaret. The physical pain of the cross was truly horrible. They even had to invent a new name for it. 'Excruciating,' meaning 'out of the cross.' And you're right; others felt the excruciating pain of crucifixion. But let me ask you this, and please don't take offense because none is intended. I just want to make a point. But what if you were to feel all the pain of one hundred cancer patients? Two hundred? One thousand? How about a million cancer patients, and all their pain was inflicted upon you?"

She seemed shocked, and I began to feel as if I had overstepped. "That's ridiculous," she answered. "That could never happen. No person could bear all of that pain. They would die within seconds in that amount of pain."

"And yet," I added softly, "that's basically what Jesus did."

"Wait a minute!" Raiders dad was actually processing the evening's activities. His daughter and I shared a quick, knowing glance. "I don't remember anything about Jesus suffering from cancer, either on his own or for anybody else."

Okay, while he threw out a weak theological argument, at least he was involved, I thought. I ventured into its simple, basic theology. "Not cancer. Sin. All the sins of every single person, ever. All mankind throughout the ages and into the future.

And through his pain, he saved every last one of us. There is nothing we can do to earn our way to Heaven and eternal life. But God has made a way for us. All we have to do is believe the Gospel and accept Jesus as our Savior."

Matthew grumbled his protest. "There it is! Here comes the Bible-thumping on top of our heads. The dreaded sin accusations! Feel guilty, all you sinners! You're a horrible person! Ain't no good in you! Don't do this, don't do that; it's a sin!"

I raised my coffee cup as if toasting his remarks, and he smirked. "Well, your nature, my nature, all of humankind's nature is, as the Bible teaches us and as we exhibit daily, sinful, not good. And there is no amount of good deeds we can do to save ourselves. But a quick question for you, Matt. What is a sin?"

He looked at me as if I was the most ignorant person he had ever met. "I just said it. It's something we do that is bad."

"Today, we look at sin in that way, for sure, and that's true, to a point. But the word 'sin' actually comes from archery. If you fire your arrow at a target and you don't hit that center bullseye, that's a sin. It means you missed the mark. That doesn't mean you are a 'bad' archer. It means you missed the mark, which we all do with God. If we don't believe in him, we've missed the mark. If you don't follow him, you've missed a mark."

The daughter of the Raiders fan quietly enjoined, "Michael, you said that all we have to do in order to be saved and have eternal life is to accept God's gift, but there is a little more to it than just accepting Jesus as your Savior. You need to recognize where you"—she looked at me with a smile of appreciation—"haven't met the mark and repent for those wrongdoings. He'll forgive you." She looked at Margaret with love and empathy in her eyes.

This made my thoughts return to Margaret. "The pain you feel of possibly leaving your children behind? He's felt it, too."

"I will be leaving them." She held back the tears, and her voice cracked. "The doctors have given me three months."

"I'll pray for you every day." Her stare showed that she believed I would. "Miracles still do happen."

She looked away. As I waited, I watched her intravenous drip line. With each silvery-clear drop of liquid, time seemed to stand still. I suddenly felt compelled to speak. So, I continued. "That pain you spoke of. The pain of leaving your children. There's another related pain to that, you know. It's the pain of having your children leave *you*. The pain of losing a child is one I know about. Mine left this earth suddenly, like Matt's friends. But there is also the pain of having a child leave and never wanting to see or talk to you again. That pain, I don't know. But both of those pains have been felt by God. Not with just one or two children, but with billions. Countless children throughout the ages and into the future. Imagine it. You don't love one child any more or less than another. Your love is unconditional. And if you lose even half of them, *that* pain would be enough to drive you mad, wouldn't it? And yet, God loses many of his children every day as they abandon him." The room suddenly seemed darker and quieter when I finished speaking.

Margaret thought and answered sadly, "Yeah. I'd be heartbroken. And in a horrible state of depression."

The daughter of the Raiders fan jumped in quickly. "Margaret, you mentioned that others were crucified and tortured by the Romans, just like Jesus was. It reminded me that in our youth group, we learned that Christ suffered before he was arrested as well. Not just the physical whipping and beatings. He went through an incredible amount of mental suffering, like when he prayed to the Father to take the cup from him. He even sweated blood, which physicians today acknowledge can happen to some people under extreme stress."

Margaret wasn't distracted from her main spiritual obstacle. "Did your youth group have an answer to the question, 'Why me,' though? Why do bad things happen to good people? Or how my suffering is a service to anyone?"

The teenage girl looked at me as if she wanted to answer Margaret, and I sensed that she was nervous and uncertain about her ability to defend and define her faith. I smiled at her and encouraged her with a head nod. A sip of my coffee told me to heat it up, so

I meandered back to the hospitality table and gave the floor to a high school believer.

"Well," she started, "our youth pastor explained to us that we should look at our problems like a test or as a way to get closer to God. To use it to seek and find him more and more. We will still make bad decisions that will lead to bad consequences, but if we recognize them and fix them in a way that will please and glorify God, then we will become that much closer to God. He said that sometimes we even find God through, or even because of, our suffering." The girl was looking Margaret squarely in the eye with compassion, love, and seriousness that I had never before seen in one so young. "I hope you do," she said sincerely. "He can bring you some peace through all the pain."

"Thanks," Margaret softened after hearing her sentiments. "I hope my girls grow up to be strong and loving teenagers like you." The girl's father took note, and he could not have looked any prouder than if his team had won the Super Bowl.

"Thanks. I appreciate that," the girl said. "But you know, you can start them on their way by setting an example. You can ask Christ into your heart. It's easy to do. You just pray and ask him to forgive you for everything you've done wrong and let him help you to turn away from those things. Ask him to come be with you. To guide you and change your heart to his will. Then let your girls know about it. Tell them why you accepted him and why it's important that they do as well. If need be, I'll be glad to help your girls anytime." She tore out a piece of blue-lined notebook paper and wrote on it. "Here's my name and phone number, along with an email address. Just call or have them contact me. I'll be glad to have them as friends and, hopefully, sisters." Her father looked at her in confusion. "In Christ, Dad. Sisters in Christ."

I was surprised at how easily this young girl evangelized Margaret but was not surprised as Margaret began to sputter, "I ... I don't know." Her cheeks flushed with red, which was nice to see, as she had previously looked so pale. Raiders fan's daughter was seemingly now at a loss for words, so I stepped in.

"Just ask for a Bible when they take you to your room. No. Wait. I'll get you one. I'll find one and bring it to you. I'll read the Gospel of Mark with you if you'd like. I have a feeling you might find his writing interesting."

"Mark?" she asked, "Why Mark? Why not John? Isn't that where the most famous verse comes from, John 3:16?"

I couldn't help but chuckle. "Margaret, when you start reading the Bible, you will be amazed at how many famous verses you have heard before or didn't even know were from the Bible and how many stories, or life lessons that you've been taught over the years, oblivious to the fact that they are biblical. But I think Mark's Gospel will grab you because Mark deals with what we've been talking about: suffering.

He spends time presenting Jesus to us as a suffering servant."

Margaret needed to study Mark. I knew that in my heart. I had already formed a short study plan for her in my mind. I pray you use it and that God will open your eyes to his glory.

As the night marched on, I grew more attached to all the people in the room. All except the lady in the far corner, who was watching all of us but not wanting to get involved. While I wanted to approach her and make sure she was all right, I would not have the opportunity to do so until my shift was over. Besides, the Raiders fan was getting a bit edgy after watching his daughter share her faith.

JESUS, THE SUFFERING SERVANT

The Gospel of Mark emphasizes Jesus' humility and willingness to endure suffering for the sake of others.

Mark 10:45:

Not to be served, but to serve.

Mark 8:31:

Jesus begins to teach his disciples about his impending suffering and death.

Mark 9:31:

Further prediction of Jesus' suffering and rejection.

Mark 10:32-34:

Jesus tells his disciples about the persecution and death he will face.

Mark 14:32-42:

The agony in the Garden of Gethsemane.

Mark 15:16-39:

The account of Jesus' crucifixion, detailing his suffering and humiliation.

BONUS: Isaiah 53:

The imagery of the suffering servant in Isaiah is seen as a prophecy fulfilled in Jesus.

QUESTIONS TO THINK ABOUT AND DISCUSS

1.   What are three concerns that the Raiders fan's daughter addressed?

2.   What other questions might Margaret ask in response to the answers the young girl gave? How might you address those new questions?

3.   Knowing Jesus Christ as the suffering servant, how can this help you answer the question of why bad things happen to good people? (Hints: Ecclesiastes 9:2, 2 Corinthians 1:3-4, The entire book of Job)

4.   Michael and the Raiders fan's daughter talk about how we can be saved and have eternal life. If you were standing before God and he asked you, "Why should I allow you to enter heaven to live with me here forever?" how would you answer? Does 1 Corinthians 15:1-7 help answer this question? Why or why not?

CHAPTER THREE

LUKE

I briefly went on to explain that John Mark, in his Gospel, while addressing many aspects of Jesus' divinity, spends quite a bit of time concentrating on persecution and martyrdom. Just as I finished, the approaching wail of a siren could be heard. We all quieted a moment as we realized that another patient was about to enter the emergency room. Matt's face went pale, and he began to fidget, the sound of that siren reminding him why he was there. The Raiders guy broke the awkwardness with a rather snide sounding, "So!" then marched forward with, "If the Gospel of Mark is the best book for Margaret here to read first, what would you say is the best one for me to read?" The question was laced with sarcasm.

I suddenly began to feel that I was, in some small manner, connecting with this guy. I also realized

I didn't know his name. "Well," I gestured for his name.

"Oh, Luke," he said, extending his hand. "Luke Kilter. Certified public accountant."

I shook his hand, wondering how I should answer. "Well, Luke," I slowly began as the four Gospels began revolving around in my mind, "turns out, reading the Bible can be a really personal thing. I've read certain scriptures numerous times. Sometimes I understand them; other times, I just don't get it, or I get confused. I can talk to my pastor or guys in my Bible study, but even then, it doesn't always register with me. Then, one day, I read a verse I've read a thousand times, and, bang! The Lord hits me with a meaning that had escaped me every other time I had read those exact same verses."

"You must have been reading the King James Version," his daughter giggled.

I laughed. "Sometimes. But you know, even the different translations of the Bible may speak to one individual more than another. Or, sometimes, it may help to clear up some verse you've been contemplating. Personally, I like the English Standard Version." I paused as I thought of Joy reading her Bible. "My wife would read the New American Standard Bible, which is much like the ESV, but she enjoyed it the best."

"See!" Luke almost threw his laptop into the air as he seemed to jump out of his seat. "That's just wrong!"

I was taken aback at his outburst and even more confused at his statement. "Wrong? Why? What are you talking about?"

He was still quite animated, and his flock of dark, straight hair seemed to fly in all directions as he gestured madly. "Because," he insisted, "you need to have all your ducks in a row!"

"Huh?" Matt appeared to have sobered up some and seemed ready to find his voice again, even if it was only a primal grunt of confusion. At least he was following the thread.

Luke glanced at Matt and started counting on his fingers, "One, two, three, four, five. It doesn't go one, two, four, three, five, does it? It doesn't matter what it is, whether you file the 1040 form or the 1040EZ paperwork. Or, let's say you have to complete a Schedule C, D, E, and F. If there's no standard protocol to follow, no logical progression, or no specific order, you're toast! If there are so many different versions of the Bible to follow, it means there are multiple choices of interpretation. There is no way you can possibly figure it all out correctly! Or even how to be a 'proper' Christian. That's why all you Christian believers are so hypocritical!"

"Dad. We're human beings, not paperwork," his daughter scoffed. Her expression was no longer playful with her father, but zealous. "This argument coming from your little bizarre CPA mind is veering toward the truth, but not in the way you're thinking.

You're right in thinking that there shouldn't be multiple ways to know the truth. The truth is, there is only one way to get it right. Jesus told us that no one gets to the Father except through him."

Luke softened to his daughter's passion, and his contention turned more toward a civilized debate and away from a heated argument. "I'm not thinking so much about what Jesus said. People say things all the time, but their actions and the way they live their life don't always match their words. And Jesus' life, or at least the records we have of it, are not orderly and consistent enough to yield the results that you and Apostle Mike here are advocating."

"First off. I'm no apostle, just a humble disciple. But, explain to me what you mean by all that?" I asked.

Luke seemed to be thinking out loud as he spoke. "Well," he pondered, "when Jesus was walking around here on Earth ... he was human, right?"

"Fully man, and fully God. Yes," I nodded.

"Because, logically, if he were human, he would have been forced to follow human ways, right? He would be subject to human emotions, human laws, and earthly laws. That means his life would have had some sort of order to it. A chronology. So why do we have all these gospels that jump around all willy-nilly and confused like? Not one of them gives an orderly account of Jesus' life. And then there's this little problem that not every line in the gospels agrees one hundred percent with each other. In my line of work, you can get some very hefty fines for that, you know."

"Give unto Caesar," Matt quietly wisecracked.

"Luke!" I snapped my fingers at the thought.

"What?" Luke asked.

"Luke," I reiterated, oblivious to the misunderstanding.

Luke raised his eyebrows and held his palms up in a gesture indicating he was right in front of me. "What?"

I finally noodled it through. "Oh! No, I mean, Luke. Luke's Gospel. You should read it first. It's not necessarily a biography of Jesus, but it is a rather orderly account of his life. Actually, Luke was like you in some ways. He liked things to be straightforward and orderly. Being a doctor, he had to think logically in order to do the best things for his patients. So, his Gospel is put into an orderly form that you might appreciate."

Luke shook his head. "I've been through it. It's just a copy and paste of the other gospels. I mean, they all repeat the same stories. I have nothing against repetition. After all, it's important in advertising, and that is what the Gospel writers are trying to do, right? Sell Jesus to everyone? It reads to me as if they were plagiarizing off of one another."

Lotus lady's right eye squinted open as she sought me out. She probably thought that Luke had pierced the Lord's Word, or at least I would not be able to defend his Word from this assault. "Well," I drawled,

"Luke does write about many of the same events recorded in the other Gospels, like healing the sick, giving sight to the blind, comforting those in need, raising dead people …"

Luke pounced. "Wait a minute. The Bible says that Jesus rose from the dead, not anyone else."

Exasperated as only a teenager can be with her father, his daughter pleaded with me, "Can you please get him a Bible, too? When you pick up one for Margaret, grab one for him, too, okay? Please?"

I smiled and winked at her. "I'm sure you and your mom can dig one up that'll suit him." Then, turning to Luke, I said, "Your daughter's pointing out in her own way that you, along with millions of other people, think you know God's Word when you only have a basic sense of it. You see, people think they know the 'important' parts of the Bible and base their beliefs and decisions on a limited but flawed understanding of its contents. You ought to read up a little more and spend some time studying the Bible, not just skimming it or reading it like a novel. Ever hear of Lazarus?"

"Lazarus? Sure … Lazarus. Of course, I have. Everyone's heard of Lazarus," Luke replied meekly.

"And why is that name famous, Dad?" his daughter pressed.

"Because," he stumbled along, trying to recover, "because … because by the way you two are looking at me, Jesus must have raised him from the dead." She and I nodded at him.

"Don't forget the little girl," Matt tossed out. All of us stared at Matt after forgetting he was there.

"What? What little girl?" Luke asked in honest disbelief as he began to realize that there had been more than one person brought back from the dead.

I let Matt answer. "Jesus brought a daughter of a temple leader, a Jewish leader, back to life, too. He ordered everyone to keep quiet about it." He made a sarcastically dramatic air quote motion as he continued. "'The Messiah secret.' He didn't want anyone to think of him as the Messiah, so he ordered them not to say anything about him raising this little girl from the dead."

"He didn't order them. He asked them. It was more of a request." Luke's daughter was defending Jesus as she would a younger sibling who had been unjustly accused.

"She's right," I said, "And I would also add, Matt, that Jesus didn't want people to think of him as a conquering soldier-king Messiah, which most Jews were expecting. And at the time he raised that little girl from death, it was still relatively early in his ministry. It was not time yet for his truth to be known."

"That's in the book of Luke?" Luke asked.

"Actually, that event is recorded in Mark's Gospel," I answered.

Luke stared at his laptop. "Okay, so obviously, I'm no Bible scholar. I'm a CPA. You two were babbling on about different Bible translations, and it sorta triggered me for some reason. All those different versions is just one reason I have trouble getting into the Bible. I don't go for all that fancy, wordy, artistic writing I see in there."

"Hence, you're a Raiders fan," Matt actually teased, eliciting a rather profane hand gesture from the Raiders fan. "I rest my case," Matt smiled.

"Listen." I held on to the word to get his full attention. "The Gospel of Luke has a strong emphasis on historical detail, as well as showing a great understanding of Jesus and those around him. Look, Luke even starts out his Gospel by pointing out that lots of people have written accounts about Jesus and how he fulfilled prophecy, performed miracles, and the like. This is why Luke tells us that he has painstakingly researched and investigated these accounts. It's like his Gospel is his final report. His conclusions. A logical, orderly culmination of the facts that he has compiled."

"Impossible. How could he have possibly done all that research without a government grant?" Then, pointing at his laptop, Luke said, "Or a computer, for that matter." His crooked smile indicated that he was trying to retreat by interjecting humor into the moment. I couldn't let him off the hook that easily, especially with his daughter urging me on with her hope-filled blue eyes.

"You know, it's funny you say that, because Luke actually addresses his Gospel to a guy named Theophilus, who very well may have been Luke's benefactor. So, maybe there was some sort of grant for

Luke to work with." I was concerned that I might be sounding more like a nerdy theologian than I really was, but I pressed on. "Maybe Theophilus bankrolled Luke's research. We don't know for sure, but it's a possibility. Still, that aside, in Luke's day, research would have run the gamut from scouring through all sorts of written accounts to interviewing eyewitnesses to the events in Jesus' life. And Luke probably questioned those eyewitnesses himself."

Luke's furrowed brow indicated he wasn't buying in. "A guy at the office, I have no idea what he fully believes, but I know he's not a Christian. Anyway, when I hear him arguing with our Christian colleague, he always pushes the point that Luke's Gospel is just a copy of Mark's Gospel, as well as Matthew's Gospel. That there is nothing original in it. So what good is it? I mean, again, in my line of work, copying can get you into tons of trouble. You gotta double-check your work." He was shaking his head, and his mop of hair shook along with it.

Trying not to sound condescending, I said, "Well, like I said, Luke starts off telling Theophilus that many others had written about Jesus. Luke doesn't say that he relied on Mark's or Matthew's reports in order to come to any conclusions. But whether he did or not, it makes your office friend's position an unfair 'no win' scenario."

"How so?" he asked.

"Well, let's face it." I showed him my palms and shrugged my shoulders. "You can't have it both ways. You can't sit there and complain that Luke has nothing new to offer, because if he did, your argument would most likely be that nobody else reported those items, and therefore, he can't be trusted. But then, if he does write about some of the same events as the other Gospel writers, you're likely to say, 'Oh, look, Luke believes in and is just copying the events that others have written, thereby trying to discredit Luke because he's plagiarizing the other writers. You won't accept the possibility that his reports are confirming evidence of other writers' claims, and then you end up questioning whether any story he wrote about that was untold in another gospel was true because no one else mentioned it. So, I take issue with the supposition of the argument."

"It's the truth of Yin and Yang." It was the lotus lady. Somewhere along the way, her transcendental transmission lines to reach nirvana were disconnected, and she had decided to interject her mystical brain power into the conversation. All heads in the room swiveled to take her in. "The real truth, the answers to all the questions that have arisen tonight are simple. All religions, all beliefs, lead to God." She sounded like an artificially intelligent drone.

Still, I was momentarily stunned. My soul felt chilled and disgusted. I almost went into attack mode, but a quiet control came over me. I steadied my gaze upon her, and then, more firmly and forcibly than I had anticipated, I heard myself say, "Ignoring that remark for now ..." As she stared me squarely in the eye, I returned to the discussion at hand. "But, there are some other interesting differences about Luke's account that many people seem to gloss over as well."

"Such as?" Luke's daughter was just as anxious to address her father's needs as I was to postpone my confrontation with Lotus Lady.

"Well, Luke wrote in the Greek language, quite eloquently, actually, and his style is such that it indicates he was more interested in reaching the Gentiles than the Jews."

"Just because he wrote in Greek?" Luke asked.

"No. It's an indicator, though. More so, what he focuses on. The reality of it all. And he seems to concentrate on portraying Jesus as a compassionate Savior more so than, say, a teacher and a healer. Though, being a doctor, Jesus' healings were quite impressive to Luke."

Luke twisted his lips. "You've lost me."

That made me smile, and I just had to say it. "And hopefully, you'll be found." He scowled at my little Christian-ese phrase, but I continued on. "Basically, Luke confronts those who read his Gospel. He tells Theophilus, 'Look, this is what happened; here are the facts. I researched this and used impeccable sources. You can even check these sources out for yourself. Now, armed with all these facts, what are you going to do about it?'"

"Do about it?" Luke was muscling up for an argument again. "What can anyone do about it? Read it, and then what? Make a decision about God based on the writings of a man?"

"Dad," his daughter knew his buttons, so I sat down and sipped my coffee. "You just rattled on a little while ago saying it's all about the facts. You're always saying you want the bottom line, just those facts. No gray areas, only black and white, right? And, I know it's hard to understand right now, but while men wrote the words down on paper, or parchment, or whatever, those men were inspired by God. By his Holy Spirit. They wrote down what God wants us to know, and God cannot lie."

"The world *is* black and white ..." he started, but his daughter stopped him in his tracks.

"No, Dad. God is black and white, not the world. It's all these perceived gray areas that have people confused, hurting, and wanting more. Everyone is looking for their purpose everywhere except where they can find it. They refuse to accept God because they've been led to believe that if they do, they are intellectually weak, need him as a crutch, or that they will lose out on all the fun in life. Believe me, Dad, if you would come to church or Sunday school with us once in a while, you'd have more fun than watching the Raiders lose." When she finished, she kept her gaze upon him, and he looked to me for a bailout.

Instead of bailing him out, I compassionately piled on. "She's right, Luke. When Luke wrote his Gospel, he wanted us to know that the things he wrote about

Jesus were true. Now, it's up to us to either believe and accept Jesus or reject him and lose what he wants us to have: eternal life. An eternal reward."

Luke weakened. He playfully nudged his daughter, "Alright. If you're so smart, little girl, prove to me that Luke's account of Jesus is an orderly account of true events, and I'll skip the opening day of the football season to go with you and Mom to church."

She slid forward in her seat and excitedly began. "Deal! Well, Luke's really concerned about how non-Jews, the Gentiles, will respond to Jesus." She stalled a little and looked to me for help as I took a bite of food. She laughed, "That's you, Dad, a Gentile."

I swallowed quickly, laughed with her, and confirmed her words. "That's right. And to accomplish this, Luke concentrates on Jesus' Messiahship. The *type* of Messiah he is, as well as on Jesus' mission. Frankly, I think Luke's goal is summed up in verses 19:9 -10."

I read the verse, and everyone listened. Even the lotus lady. The discussion became lively, and I began to get a warm feeling about Luke. Not the Gospel writer. The guy in the waiting room. I sensed his heart was softening towards the Word of God and that he would keep his promise to his daughter to head to church as a family for opening day's kick-off, that he might even experience the Bible as he never had before. In fact, I offered up a little study for him to pursue. I include it here: Start with verse

19:9-10 of Luke's Gospel, as I did that Christmas Eve, and as you read, allow the Holy Spirit to lead you forward.

Of course, during these events, I knew that eventually, I would have to address the lotus lady. I also could not help but notice the timid lady was still engaged and listening, all the while keeping her distance. But right now, it was still Luke's turn. His daughter and I gave him a lot to ponder. Even Matt seemed to respond to Luke's Gospel in a positive way. I prayed for everyone in that room to understand what God wants us all to know: that he wants us all to come be with him, and he has lit that narrow path for us to follow. I pray that for you as well. Pick up the map and find the way. Find the light. Find the truth.

JESUS AS THE COMPASSIONATE SAVIOR

Luke's Gospel frequently depicts Jesus showing compassion toward those often overlooked in society, such as women, the poor, and sinners.

Luke 7:13:
Jesus shows compassion to a grieving widow and raises her son from the dead.
Luke 15:11-32:
The prodigal son parable. Highlights a father's immense compassion for his son.
Luke 23:28:
Tells people to not weep for him, but for themselves and their children.
Luke 19:9-10:
Jesus tells how he has come to bring salvation to the lost.

QUESTIONS TO THINK ABOUT AND DISCUSS

1.   Michael talks about Jesus being fully man and fully God. Why do you think God came down to us in this manner? Why would that be helpful to us?

2.   Take a look at Isaiah 49:13 and Psalms 86:15, 103:8, and 145:8. How do these verses point to Jesus being a compassionate Savior?

3.   Michael points out how Jesus is a compassionate Savior. What do you think the Jews of Jesus' day were expecting the Messiah to do? How does Luke's Gospel dispel this idea?

CHAPTER FOUR

ORGANIC JOHN

Organic John. Did your eyebrows raise a little? Could it be some type of organically raised Farmer John sausage? Or, if you are a Christian believer, do you think this part of the story has to do with the organic growth of Jesus' church? Organic John? Could I be poking fun at, arguably, the most important and widely quoted Gospel in the Bible? Organic John sounds more like a naturalist's outhouse than the title to a story with spiritual overtones, doesn't it? Still, the conversation that commenced with the person, whom I had previously thought of as "the lotus lady," was so surreal that I can think of no better heading.

Luke's daughter was in the middle of defending evangelistic Christians to her dad when lotus lady, who had been sitting there quiescently playing with some crystals, began to steam much like a geyser does before it finally bursts forth from the depths. "So, you see, Dad, our beliefs and convictions are backed up by the changes we see in our lives as well as the changes in the feelings we have inside ourselves. I mean, if I go see a PG-13 rated movie now, I feel kinda uncomfortable at the language or a sex scene that does nothing to further the plot or character development. It's as if God is there with me, and I know he would not want to be there listening or watching that. I may still enjoy the overall movie, but I'd enjoy it more without that stuff in it."

Suddenly booming forth as from the depths of hell, the lotus lady spouted off. "Excuse me! I am trying to reach my center here."

Everyone jumped, and Luke spoke for us all as he incredulously grunted out, "Huh?"

"I am trying to go deep into my transcendental center in order to commune with the naturalistic oneness of all," she answered, then followed up with a three-second moaning hum and the words, "God I am. Serenity now. God I am."

As we all looked at one another, amused and confused, Luke smiled and said, "Again, I ask. Huh?"

"All this talk about Jesus, the Bible, and prophecy," she spoke, waving her hands with the air of a queen wishing her people to eat cake, "merely shows that you have not been lifted to an enlightened level yet. You have yet to reach a position where you can understand the fact that Jesus was an enlightened one, that he had reached full maturity. Unlike you"—

she paused briefly to collect her thoughts—"and me. To a point. You need to understand that Jesus had already lived enough lives, thereby learning from experiencing all of the life-universe and what it has to offer."

Matt looked at me, raised his hands, and pronounced, "And now we delve into the wonderful world of religion, part two! The Woodstock faith."

Playing along with Matt, I jokingly fired back, "At least they were The *Grateful* Dead, not the reincarnated lives." I turned to the lotus lady. "I'm sorry, Miss?"

"I'm called Organna. Please, don't insult me with 'Miss.' I have no last name, either. Just Organna." It was said in a way that let me know that there would be no questioning that statement.

Luke's daughter, however, couldn't resist, "Oh! Like Shaggy, or Jewel."

Matt spritely played along, too. "Or Prince. Or rather, the artist formerly known as Prince. And then known again as Prince. Or something like that."

The daughter screwed her face a bit and told Matt, "That's like thirteen words or something, isn't it?"

I chuckled quietly and looked right back into Organna's eyes. "Okay, look, I apologize if we interfered with your meditations, Organna. But could you please tell me how it is that you know me, or anyone else here, is not enlightened?"

Organna wrinkled her nose like a five-year-old encountering a kale salad for the first time. "It's totally obvious, by listening to all these ignorant, non-enlightened discussions you all have been engaging in. All this foolish talk about an antiquated religion."

I wasn't shocked, nor was I offended. So, I replied as enlighteningly as possible. "Antiquated? You know, the Ten Commandments are older than the New Covenant of Jesus Christ, and the last time I looked, they were still good to go. Can you tell me what about them is outdated?"

Margaret chuckled through her pain. "I'm betting on the free love argument here."

Organna took her seriously, though, saying, "Oh no, there are too many other issues tied to that. Like disease, paternity, abortion. No, those are experiences none of you are properly illuminated to discuss rationally."

I pressed her. "Okay, Organna, what then? Which of the Ten Commandments should we disregard? Illuminate us."

She jumped in immediately, "That's an easy answer. Probably the most offensive commandment would be to honor your father and mother. My father was a drunken loser. Not worthy of my, or anyone's, respect or love."

I slowly nodded. "I understand. My mother raised me and my four brothers by herself after my father abandoned us for a life on skid row."

Organna, perhaps feeling the aura of her enlightenedness, almost shouted in triumph. "So, you agree with me!"

"No, not all." Luke's daughter threw me a questioning and surprised glance. "You see, Organna, the fifth commandment, 'Honor thy mother and father,' is easy for those of us who have had loving, caring parents. But for those of us who have had abusive parents, or parents that have done or continue to do dishonorable things... well... for us... the challenge is to honor our parents as far as the relationship will allow. All the while, we have to keep watch on our hearts so we don't repay them with another evil in retaliation for the hurt and wrongs they have put upon us. It's a difficult line. It would be wrong if we allowed a broken relationship to continue unattended when it might be ready to be restored. But it's also very important that we don't allow ourselves to be in an unhealthy and unbiblical relationship with a person who will only abuse us."

She didn't hesitate. "That might be easy for you."

Just as quickly, I interrupted her, "I didn't say it was easy."

"Easy or not," she posited, "in the grand scheme of the universe, it's not about forgiveness per se. In order for us to reach a higher plane, this pain inflicted upon us by our parents is just another experience we must have. We need to experience all that life is: wealth, poverty, murder, sickness..."

Luke was incredulous. "Whoa! Slow down, young lady. Murder? I have to go get myself murdered?"

Matt waved his hand knowingly. "Oh, it gets better. There is the opposite option as well. You might need to go and murder someone."

Organna, realizing how this was beginning to sound to us unknowing, unenlightened, lower-level scrubs, answered flatly, "Well, yes, sort of. Once you become enlightened, however, you will realize that not only should we all love one another, we already love one another, because we are all one." She smiled broadly. "God I am."

Luke muttered to his daughter, "I guess I'm not ready to be enlightened."

Organna addressed Luke, "It's kind of about equality. We are all equal, and everything has to level out for complete eternal harmony. Take Matt's suggestion of going out to kill someone, for example. Let's say you were murdered in a previous life. You would need to come back and murder someone. In this way, you are able to experience both sides of the issue. It's these experiences that make us whole. Of course, murder is the extreme example."

"An extreme example of lunacy," Luke snorted. "So, does this mean that you are here waiting to see if your murder victim survives so you can float to the next plane?"

Organna lowered her gaze. "No. My significant other was having an assisted out-of-body experience, and the peyote prescription was a little strong."

"Here in this antiquated world, we call that a drug overdose," Matt informed her.

"Or possibly a felony," Luke added.

Ever defiant, Organna quipped, "My partner's situation has no bearing on the truth of what we are discussing here. People who believe in the Bible are still searching for true enlightenment."

"Oh, Organna," I said compassionately. I refocused the conversation back to the truth of Jesus. "I'd argue that we Bible-reading, Bible-believing Christians *have* found it, and those who think they have to live multiple lives for enlightenment and understanding are the ones searching. Constantly searching until there is no more time to search. What if you're wrong? What if, when you die, you don't come back to experience the opposite of what you just lived?"

Before Organna could answer, Margaret jumped in. "Wait a minute. Excuse me, Organna. Are you suggesting that I wanted this cancer? That I *chose* to be inflicted with it? That I needed it to become whole?"

Organna paused for a beat or two, then tried to answer with her "enlightened truth" as inoffensively as possible. "I know at this point in your quest, it seems odd. And right now, at this moment in time, you can't, won't, or may not be able to see it. But, that's only because you're not at an enlightened enough level yet. Which means your emotions won't let you understand. Maybe in a previous life, you were a doctor that helped cancer patients, and now you want to see what it's like to be a cancer patient."

Margaret's eyes narrowed as the entire room shifted in an uncomfortably disgusted way. "I'm pretty sure oncologists deal with enough cancer patients to have a pretty good idea what it's like."

Before things really became heated, I corralled Organna's attention. "How about this, Organna? You claim we come back for multiple lives." Organna gave an emphatic nod, and I continued.

"Okay, let me ask you three questions: One, how do we know when we have experienced every possible scenario in life? Who's keeping count? Two, why don't we just make ourselves experience everything right now while we're here? Or better yet, why don't we raise ourselves from the grave, just like Jesus did? That way, we don't have to waste time with all the growing up and all. We can get right to the experiences we need. And finally," I held up three fingers, "three. If each of us is a small part of the whole, where is our individuality? What makes you, you? Or me, me? Aren't you making each of us a single drop of water being dropped into an ocean? Just to disappear and be integrated into a giant single organism? We would lose all of what we are, what you claim we are attempting to be. Jesus accepts us as the individuals he created us to be."

Organna's contempt at hearing the name of Jesus was palpable. "There you go again! Do you really believe all that? What proof do you have that causes you to believe in the deity of just one man, Jesus of Nazareth?"

And there it was. The opening that started a discussion that would go to the end of my shift. With the Word of God on my side, I was able to debate whether or not people would be willing to die for the truth or a lie. I pointed her to several references that detailed the truth of what Jesus endured and the odds that he could have survived it, and yet after all the torture and after his horrible death upon the cross, he was seen by numerous people after he rose from the grave. Organna never answered the question as to what the consequences would be if she was wrong. That is a question every person should answer. The answer that a Christian can give to that question is much more appealing than any other religious worldview can give.

I encourage you to seek out literature by medical experts that entails what Jesus endured for us. In addition, I'll put in some of the Bible verses I mentioned during the Organna episode.

JESUS AS THE RISEN SAVIOR
AND THE SON OF GOD

The primary verses in John's Gospel about Jesus as the Risen Savior are John 20:1-29.

John 20:11-18:
Jesus appears to Mary Magdalene and the disciples.
John 20:19-23:
The appearance to the disciples in the locked room.
John 20:24-29:
The doubting Thomas story.
John 11:25-26:
Jesus declares: "I am the resurrection and the life."

THE GOSPEL OF JOHN TELLS US THAT
JESUS IS THE SON OF GOD

John 1:34:
John the Baptist bears witness.
John 11:27:
Martha calls Jesus Messiah and Son of God.
1 John 5:12:
States that those who have the Son have eternal life.
John 1:49:
Nathanael answers Jesus that he is the Son of God.

QUESTIONS TO THINK ABOUT AND DISCUSS

1. Organna says Christianity is an antiquated religion. What is her reasoning for this thought? What points can be made that Christianity is not an outdated worldview and is as relevant today as it was two thousand years ago?

2. How might Organna respond to the first of the Ten Commandments: You shall have no other gods before Me?

3. Organna mentions the need to live through different life experiences in order to reach "enlightenment." How would you respond to the accusation that God's plans do not even out our lives, that he and his plans are not fair? (Hint: Psalm 73:12-20, Romans 9:14-15)

4. Michael asks Organna the question, "What if you're wrong?" How might followers of these worldview beliefs answer that question? 1) New Ageism, 2) Atheism, 3) Islam, 4) Buddhism, 5) Christianity.

CHAPTER FIVE

IT IS FINISHED

After a lively, seemingly all-encompassing theological discussion in which everyone seemed to participate at some point, a nurse came to take Margaret back to the treatment area of the emergency room. All of us quieted momentarily and watched as they wheeled her out of the waiting room. While the others wished her luck and all the best, Luke's daughter and I told her we would be praying for her and her children. She smiled and waved farewell to the room. As she crossed through the doorway, I turned back to the others who were still waiting. "Well, I thank you all for listening to me and for the spirited discussion. You guys made the rest of my shift the best part of my day."

Matt laughed, "Ya, rental copping isn't always very exciting, huh?"

"Oh, you'd be surprised, Matt," I responded, "especially in a hospital. You see, violence is not unheard of here. Physical resistance to care and treatment is commonplace. Not to mention, we do get prisoners transported here occasionally. And while guards obviously come with them, we do have to be vigilant as to who might walk in those doors and cause trouble for those guys. Anyway, my shift's over, and it's time for me to head on home. If any of you want to talk more about the joy that Jesus Christ can bring you, there are plenty of folks you can ask. And"—I looked at Matt with a playful smile while waving my business cards at him—"I actually have a few of my 'rent-a-cop' business cards I'll leave right here by the coffee pot. Feel free to contact me anytime. Merry Christmas to you all. Just remember to take a moment and realize that none of these conversations would have taken place tonight if Christ had not been born, lived his life the way he did, and sacrificed his life so all of us could live."

Organna smoldered, then actually smiled. "I'll astrally project to you later, just to help set you on the right path."

I smiled right back at her. "Oh, Organna. I know the path that is wide, like an astral plane. And I know the path that is narrow that leads to life, true eternal life. I choose the narrow one. I pray you find its trailhead as well."

She just shook her head.

Luke's daughter jumped up, crossed the room, and gave me a huge bear hug. Luke watched and gave me an approving nod. "Thank you." She whispered. "This is the best my dad has ever listened to the good news."

"Oh, don't thank me; you know who deserves the thanks," I said, winking at her. "Hey, you know, I never got your name, buddy."

"Joy," she beamed.

My heart was full as I smiled down at her, "Of course it is. Joy. Anyway, you know I'm not the one to thank." I pointed up. "He is. And he's the one you and I have to keep praying to about your dad. God gave you to your dad for a reason. I suspect both of you will do great things. And when you do, never forget to glorify him." I pointed upward one more time. She gave me another hug and went and sat by her father.

I grabbed my coat and headed to the door that led to the lockers, where I had stored my personal items during my shift. A small voice behind me forced me to turn back. "Excuse me. Michael?" It was the quiet lady who had been listening and watching from a distance but always looked away when I glanced at her.

"Yes, ma'am? Is everything alright?" I asked, thinking this was going to be a security hospitality thing.

"I couldn't help but listen to the conversations going on in there," she said, motioning to the waiting room. "And, well, I have a question. It's dumb because I pretty much know what your answer will be but..." She stalled out and looked absently at the wall.

I brought her back with, "Hey, you know that old saying: 'There are no dumb questions.'"

She smiled. "Pretty sure I asked some pretty stupid ones while I was in high school. But in this case, it seems silly because I know the answer, but..." she stalled again.

"No worries. What has you crossed up?" I asked.

She sighed. "Does God really give second chances? I mean, would he use a miracle to save someone nowadays?"

I smiled as I replied, "I believe he gives way more than just a second chance. Jesus came down to Earth to save us. He knows we are far from perfect and can never do enough on our own to be worthy of him. So, he came to rescue us from the prison we have put ourselves in. He came to free us from our chains to this world and to encourage us to have a one-on-one relationship with him. Once we believe that, understand that, and work into that faith with him, we will want to learn even more about him. Once we get there, we will realize how many chances he has given us just to get to that point."

She nodded. "I get that. I mean, I study the Bible with a few other ladies in my church, so I know all that. But... I guess... I mean... Could he heal that lady with cancer you were talking with, so she could believe in him?"

"The easy answer is God can do anything he wants, right?" I smiled at her. "But, I'm not really sure what you're asking. Are you asking about healing, miracles, or what?"

She bit her lip and paused. "My dad is currently undergoing an MRI of his brain. He's been in a coma for 3 months. He's an atheist, and he'll be mad, but I have prayed for him every day to wake up. And before the coma, I prayed he would drop his faith in nothing and man and believe in God. To find Christ."

I eyed her in confusion as we both sat down. "Okay. But I guess I don't see where you're going with this."

She looked me square in the eyes. "I was reading to him in Luke chapter 16, verses 19-31. You know, the parable where Jesus talks about the two men who die? The rich guy and the poor guy? And where they end up?" I nodded, and she continued. "Well, when I finished reading the parable to him, I began to pray. Sitting there by his side, I prayed that, somehow, while Dad was in his coma, God could reach my father and turn his heart to the truth. That God could ... would... save my dad before he died in his comatose state." She looked down, almost as if she were ashamed.

I quickly said, "That's a beautiful thing to pray. Your father is still alive, and while you don't know his heart like God does, there is always hope. Coma or no coma."

I misjudged. She wasn't ashamed; she was in awe. She looked me in the eye once again. "He woke up right at the end of my prayer."

"That's fabulous!" I declared. "Praise the Lord!"

"Yes," she beamed. "But what if my dad still won't believe? I mean, it's God giving a second chance, right? Bringing someone out of a coma that was pronounced brain dead? What if my dad refuses to believe it was a miracle? A second chance for him?"

I took a deep breath. "Look, I don't claim to know the mind or the ways or the whys of God. I do know that he loves every single one of us and doesn't want any of us to perish. He wants us to be able to share in the joy of him forever." I caught my breath and started again. "I don't really know the answer to your question. There may be other reasons he woke up your father. Maybe to strengthen you and give you more faith in your prayer life. Maybe to grab the attention of the doctors and nurses that have attended to your father's care. Maybe some reason neither of us can fathom because it is beyond our sight and understanding. But it *is* a second chance for your father. A second chance that hopefully he will take and become a believer in Jesus Christ. So, I think, maybe, God already answered your question, didn't he? And it's not a dumb question. While in your heart, you knew that you never really had to ask it of me, it was definitely a question to which you needed the answer reaffirmed. Yes, God gives second chances and so much more."

"I know," she whispered. "I'm just having trouble believing it. I'm so scared that I will blow it. What if I can't convince my dad that God did this for him?"

"That's not for you to worry about. The decision is

your father's, and you are not the one to make it for him or to convince him." She lowered her eyebrows in a confused manner. "You do need to tell him what happened. You can tell him about all the people who prayed for him and even have them visit to show their love for him. But it's God's Holy Spirit who will work on him. This decision is between your father and God. You can help your dad to understand God's word and God's plan, but you can't believe it for him. Let God work."

She held out both her hands, and I took them in mine. She prayed without hesitation. "Father God, I have no words but thank you. Please help me to help my father find you. Thank you for bringing me down here to listen to all the conversations that you made possible tonight. I know there are no coincidences. You know everything that is going to happen, and you set courses for us to follow if we will only trust you and follow your lead. Amen." She surprised me with a hug, looked me once more in the eyes, and said, "I have to go see if Dad's back in his room." She winked, smiled, patted me on the shoulder, and said, "Onward, Christian soldier."

As she headed to the elevator, I once again bade farewell to everyone in the waiting room and continued my trek to gather my things and head home. It was a chilly night, and as I walked to my car, I marveled at the beauty of the small snow flurries blowing about. A long-lost childhood memory surfaced. A night much like tonight, when I was around eight years old. My dad and I went to the car to sneak in the presents he and I had bought for my mom and sisters. My dad told me how proud he was of me that I was able to keep all these presents a secret from them. Immediately, my thoughts went to my heavenly Father. I silently thanked him for the people he put in front of me tonight. I told him I hoped that I had made him proud for *not* keeping *him* a secret. I reached my car and thanked him again when my temperamental vehicle actually turned over and started.

As I pulled out, I felt it more than I saw it. There was a shimmer in my peripheral vision. I slammed on the brakes. The hind end of my vehicle swapped with its front end. As my merry-go-round car spun, I caught a glimpse of what seemed like a monster truck whizzing past. My car came to rest on the side of the road, right in front of a blow-up nativity decoration. I laughed shakily as the juvenile-looking Joseph seemed to sway and wave at me. I stepped out of my car just as some of my security buddies came running across the street. They joked a lot about calling ambulances, getting a gurney from the emergency room hallway, and, of course, asking if I was right with God, just in case I didn't survive another close call. I pointed to the blow-up nativity in all its blazing glory and told them, "This ain't my first Christmas Eve, boys, and I pray he gives me many more just like this one. Without the thrill ride."

Then I remembered the promise I made to Margaret. "Hey, guys," I playfully ordered my fellow rent-a-cops, "help me get this beater out of the snowbank. I have a date with a friend back in the ER." In between all the elbowing and teasing, we managed to get my car out, and I slowly maneuvered it back into its parking space. I looked at Joy's Bible in the backseat. With a sigh and a smile, I grabbed it and headed back in to see Margaret.

GOD WANTS TO SAVE EVERYONE, EVERY SINNER

1 Timothy 2:4
2 Peter 3:9
Ezekiel 18:23

GOD'S PLAN FOR ALL PEOPLE

Isaiah 41:10:
God will strengthen, help, and uphold people.
Jeremiah 29:11:
God has plans for people's welfare and to give them a future and hope.
Romans 8:28:
God's plans are for all things to work together for the good of those who love God.

QUESTIONS TO THINK ABOUT AND DISCUSS

1.   The believing lady speaking to Michael said she knew the answer to her question, so why did she need his answer? Have you ever doubted God or his written word? How did you eventually deal with this doubt?

2.   Michael tells the lady to leave it to God to work on her father for his salvation. What should your part be if a friend or family member is not a believer?

3.   Read 1 Peter 2:11-3:16. Does this cause you to reconsider your answer to question number two or strengthen your resolve to keep it?

4.   While not spoken of directly, the Trinity is shown to play a part in this woman's story. How would you explain to someone how each person in the Godhead—Father, Son, and Holy Spirit—played a part in her father's miracle?

FIVE IN WAITING-
ORIGINAL SCRIPTS

The following pages contain the original four drama scripts that inspired the novella, Five in Waiting: Conversations of Faith in the E.R. I include them here not only because many people enjoy reading a script type format, but also for anyone considering teaching the subject matter. Utilizing drama, live or through video production, can help to engage your audience and create an environment in which they are more receptive to your message. As they absorb the drama taking place in front of them, they not only retain the material that may have touched them, but they also become prepared and interested in what the message will be. This can translate into more attentive and, hopefully, more receptive minds.

If you wish to use these scripts to stage productions in your church, please feel free to do so. I give you permission. No extra fee, no royalty payments. If you wish to make any changes that you feel will make it more engaging for your church or audience, please do so. For example, you will notice during one of Luke's daughter's speeches, she mentions her youth pastor, Christian. The youth pastor of the church in which these skits were first performed was indeed named "Christian." He did like to surf and, at the time, he was known to crash while ice skating. These personal touches not only bring a smile and chuckle to many in the congregation, they also make them feel more involved in the moment. They realize the scenes playing out in front of them were designed for them, and they appreciate it.

I hope you are able to use these little dramas as is, or as a template to glorify God. When you do, remember throughout the production process to do everything with joy for the Lord!

CAST OF CHARACTERS

MICHAEL: the off-duty security guard.
            A Christian, kindly man who
            facilitates the discussions.

MATT: the graduate student that has
            been to a Christmas party, is
            slightly intoxicated, and is
            there because of a car wreck. He
            should have some bandages on, and
            cuts, etc. Two of his friends
            were killed in the crash, and one
            is clinging to life. He is tired
            of "religion."

MARGARET: the cancer patient. In the
            emergency room because of a
            reaction to the chemo/radiation
            therapy. She is suffering.

LUKE: the accountant. He's a regular
            joe who likes order in life.

DAUGHTER: teenage daughter of Luke that
            is a believer, along with her
            mother, who is at the emergency
            room for an injury.

ORGANNA: the new-ager. She is a 60's
            type throwback, but not to be
            played over-the-top. She will
            be in a lotus yoga position and
            meditating. She has several
            colorful crystals on the floor
            before her. She occasionally
            rotates, kisses them, moves them
            around, then returns to her
            "meditation." She does, however,
            pay attention to the discussions.

<u>SCENE</u>

A hospital emergency waiting room on
Christmas Eve.

Setting: A couple of couches,
             chairs, end tables with
             magazines, and worldly
             Christmas decorations. A
             coffee maker with styrofoam
             cups, etc., although
             MICHAEL should have his
             own travel cup. The video
             screens exhibit the words,
             "CHRISTMAS EVE," that
             slowly fade out. After
             the text fades, there can
             be a photo of a hospital
             emergency sign, perhaps
             using a local hospital if
             permission is granted.
             All but Michael and Matt
             are seated, doing various
             "waiting" activities.

GOSPEL OF MATTHEW SKETCH

(WEEKEND ONE IN DECEMBER)

MICHAEL

(Michael enters, surveys
the scene, and heads to
the coffee maker with his
lunch pail. Looks at others
and gestures to all about
coffee)

While I'm here...anyone want a cup of
Cuppa Joe?

(All shake head "no," except
for LUKE)

LUKE

Yeah, I could use another boost. Looks
like I'm in for a long wait; might as
well be wired for it.

MICHAEL

How long have you been waiting?

LUKE

About an hour. They just took my wife
back for x-rays and...

(LUKE stares as MATT enters
with a backpack, dragging.
He is swaying ever so

slightly and is banged up.)

MICHAEL

(To MATT)

Coffee's on me, son. Need a cup?

MATT

(Angrily)

Look, I don't need a lecture. OK?

(Michael begins to try to speak)

Yes! We were out drinking. OK?! Offering me a cup of coffee to sober me up... Ha, Ha. Very funny. Well, your stupid little joke isn't going to help anything.

MICHAEL

Sorry, son. I was just offering...

MATT

And I'm not your son! My name's Matt. And I don't need any more sobering up. I'm as sober as a judge, now ...

(calms a bit)

Seeing two of your best friends die, and having another on life support has a way of doing that.

MICHAEL

(looks to LUKE, who is now anxiously working on his

> laptop; ORGANNA has closed
> her eyes in meditation;
> DAUGHTER calmly watches,
> and MARGARET appears
> sympathetic. MICHAEL and
> MATT head to chairs)

Look, I'm sorry, Matt. About your friends—I really wasn't insinuating anything. I really was just offering you some coffee, as I did everyone else.

> (DAUGHTER nods)

Look. I work here every night... I never really know what everyone's story is, but on my lunch hour and at the end of my shift—I know it sounds weird—but I like to come in here and see if I can help make the wait a little easier for everyone.

MATT

Oh, so you're a rent-a-cop, and a SHRINK?

MICHAEL

No. But instead of looking for someone to vent on, maybe you ought to be thanking God that you're in this room and not in the one back there.

> (Points to the hospital
> doors)

MATT

Thank? Listen. I'd rather be back
there... I'd trade spots with Lance
back there in a heartbeat!... He
didn't even want to go with us. I
talked him into it! He just got
married.

(Beat)

I ought to be the one back there, not
him.

MICHAEL

Well, that's noble of you, son. But
I'm sure there are a lot of people,
who, while grieving the loss of your
friends and praying for Lance, are
pretty happy that you're alright.

MATT

(waving it off)

Naw. No one really.

MICHAEL

I know one.

(Matt looks up at Michael,
rather surprised he could
know any of his friends.)

Jesus is.

MATT

(Throws hands up in the air
in disgust)

Oh, great! A rent-a-cop, a shrink, and

now a religious Bible thumper! Look, Columbo, I'm a graduate student at U.C. Berkeley... I've taken classes on ...

(counts on his fingers)

... world religions, philosophy, astrology, anthropology, biology and evolution, as well as a plethora of other subjects. Don't even start trying to comfort me with religion.

MICHAEL

I'm not talking about Religion, Matt. I'm talking about Christianity.

MARGARET

Sorry to interrupt, Mr.?

(As she looks at MICHAEL, she indicates she is searching for a name).

MICHAEL

Michael.

MARGARET

Michael... But Christianity is a religion … at least the last time I looked it was.

MATT

See? She can figure it out, and she's probably a GED candidate.

MICHAEL

(To MARGARET)

Not really... You see, religion is
humans trying to work their way to
God. Christianity is God coming to men
and women through a relationship with
Jesus Christ.

LUKE

Same difference. That's Christian-
ese double speak. Talk like that
infiltrates people's minds and it
causes people to throw their hands
up in church, making everyone
uncomfortable.

DAUGHTER

Excuse me!?

(As she looks at her dad)

Ok Dad. Try to guess who I am now.
TOUCHDOWN RAIDERS!

(She leaps into the air off
her seat, throws her arms
up in the air and dances
around.)

LUKE

(stares at her for a beat)

THAT'S different. That's sports. Uh...
an exciting... spur of the moment
kinda thing.

DAUGHTER

Oh. I see … and people in church, having a spiritual moment with God, their Creator... is not an exciting spur of the moment thing... A sports moment is more worthy of that type of behavior? More worthy of your praise and worship?

ORGANNA

(As Luke stares at his daughter, slightly embarrassed)

Well, when the Raiders score, it is a small miracle.

(Goes right back to meditation as all stare at her for a beat)

MATT

Yeah … Well... when it comes to religion, been there, done that. I was raised in the Jewish religion. I tried the others. I've been dunked, sprayed, splashed, sprinkled, doused, hosed down... you name it. And where did it get me? In an emergency room with two dead friends, and one more clinging to life.

(hangs head)

MARGARET

And you, very much alive.

MICHAEL

And thank God for that, Matt.... You
have a second chance.... All you've
been through tonight. The fear,
the frustration, the loss, and the
grief. It need not be in vain. Always
remember, Christ came to save you; he
wants a relationship with you.

                    MATT

Christ?

              (disgustedly)

Look... My professor for World
Religions said that there's no proof
Jesus was anything more than a great
teacher... He didn't even make it
to prophet status. And as for Jesus
being the Messiah? My father, a Jew,
spoke of a messianic age.... Not an
individual messiah. In fact, he showed
me how not even half of the prophecies
were fulfilled by Jesus. Sorry to burst
your bubble, Ranger Mike, but Jesus
didn't fit the bill to be the Christ.

                  ORGANNA

Ah... Prophecies! There are so many
other questions that need answering as
well... But go ahead, Michael... What
of the prophecy fulfillment? Hmmm?

                  MICHAEL

Well,

              (As he begins to answer, all
              freeze.)

83

PASTOR MESSAGE HERE. ANOTHER QUESTION MAY BE INCORPORATED HERE PER PASTOR'S REQUEST.

GOSPEL OF MARK SKETCH

(WEEKEND TWO IN DECEMBER)

The scene is as before, picking up as if MICHAEL has finished answering the prophecy question.

MICHAEL

So, there you have it. The probabilities of the prophecies being fulfilled by one man, in Jesus, are astounding. And they were not realized to be fulfilled until after his death....after his resurrection, and ascension... Which is one of the reasons Jews at that time felt that many prophecies went unfulfilled.

MARGARET

(Winces in pain as she leans forward to talk)

But, prophecies are one thing, morality is another.

MICHAEL

I don't follow you.

MARGARET

I'm a single mother of two. I'm here because of a reaction I'm having to the chemo and radiation treatments I've been getting... So my question is... Why ME? I'm a good person. I mean, I can deal with my pain to a point. I suffer through it.... But why would God have my children suffer, too? My parents are gone, I was an only child... and now I'm looking for someone to love and care for them when I die. The pain I feel for my girls is worse than the pain of this cancer.

LUKE

(Looking the other way and somewhat to himself)

The age old question: Why do bad things happen to good people?

MICHAEL

Well, It's obvious that you're a strong person, even though you're weakened by cancer. Before I try to answer that, may I pray for you and your kids?

(MARGARET stares at him for a beat or two, and then looks away with a nod)

I'm sorry. I didn't catch your name.

MARGARET

Margaret. Margaret Marks.

MICHAEL

(Bows head to pray, along with DAUGHTER, and MARGARET. LUKE watches, while MATT impatiently leans Back. ORGANNA shuffles her crystals

                and "poofs" her hands at
                MARGARET)

Lord God. We lift up Margaret to
you today. We ask you to place your
healing hand upon her, and if it is
your will, remove this cancer that
she has bravely been fighting. Help the
doctors to find the correct treatments
and ease her pain—the pain from the
cancer, the pain from her life, and
the pain and worry she has for her
children. Ease her suffering, Lord.
You, Lord, the Son that has suffered
the most, can understand her pain
and suffering, and comfort her at
this time. Lord Jesus, we know that
your greatest suffering was also the
greatest service to us of all time.
And we ask you to be with Margaret
and her children and comfort them, in
their time of suffering... to look
over them. We ask that you give her
children the strength and courage they
will need in the days ahead, that
you will comfort them in their times
of sorrow and fear. Finally, Lord,
we ask that if it be necessary, you
find a good and loving home, a family
that will love and care for them. We
pray this in the name of our precious
savior, Jesus Christ. Amen.

                MARGARET

Thank you.

                (Beat)

But I noticed while you were praying that you said Jesus had suffered the most. I'm sure the pain on the cross was awful, but others were crucified at those times... How was his suffering any worse than theirs, or other people that were beaten and tortured?

DAUGHTER

Because he suffered the suffering of ALL of us.

(all look at her surprised. Then after she looks at each one, ending on her father)

MICHAEL

Impressive. I'm pretty sure they don't teach that theology in public schools, where . . .

LUKE

Her mother takes her to church.

MICHAEL

(More statement than question)

And you don't go with them.

DAUGHTER

(As LUKE waves Michael off)

Someday he will. He doesn't know it yet, but he will. The whole church is praying for him.

> (LUKE looks at her in mock
> horror)

Right now, he worships at the altar of
the Las Vegas Raiders on Sunday.

LUKE

"Just win Baby!" Raiders 3:16

MATT

(Off-handed)

Not sure even prayer can help them...

MICHAEL

(to MARGARET)

She's right, you know. The physical
pain of the cross was horrible...They
even had to invent a new name for it:
"excruciating." Meaning, "out of the
cross." And you're right; others felt
the physical pain of crucifixion. But
let me ask you this, and please don't
take offense: But what if you were
to feel all the pain of 100 cancer
patients? Two hundred? One thousand?
One million?

MARGARET

That's ridiculous. That could never
happen … No person could bear
all that. They would die within
milliseconds with that amount of pain.

MICHAEL

And yet, that is basically what Jesus did.

LUKE

I don't remember anything about Jesus suffering from cancer. Either on his own, or for anyone else.

MICHAEL

Not cancer. Sin. All the sin of all the people, of all mankind throughout the ages. And through his pain, he saved all of us... all we need to do is accept his gift and believe. Margaret, the pain you feel of possibly leaving your children behind, he's felt that too...

MARGARET

(Sadly)

I will be leaving them. The doctors gave me three months.

MICHAEL

I will pray for you every day. I believe that God does miracles still today. But the pain of leaving them— or worse still, if they leave you—the pain of losing a child is one I can not even imagine. But now, imagine it's not just two children, but millions, billions, countless children through the ages. You don't love one any more or less than any other; your love is unconditional. And you lose them. That pain would be enough to drive you mad, wouldn't it? God loses many of his children every day as they abandon him.

MARGARET

Yeah... I'd be heartbroken, and crazy.

DAUGHTER

In our youth group we learned about Christ's suffering before he was arrested too. There was a mental suffering when he asked God to take the cup from him.

MARGARET

Did your youth group answer the question of why me? Why bad things happen to good people? And how can my suffering be a service to anyone?

DAUGHTER

(Looks to MICHAEL who nods and shows a palm as if to gesture "go ahead".)

Well.... My youth pastor, Christian...

MATT

We know he's a Christian, Missy... or he wouldn't be talking about Jesus!

DAUGHTER

No... I mean, yes... he is a Christian, obviously. But that's his name, too. Christian.

                    LUKE

               (To MATT)

Like Hans Christian Anderson.

                  DAUGHTER

Yeah, but he's better on a surfboard than he is on ice skates. Kind of a dork on the ice... Anyway, Christian explained to us that sometimes when bad things are happening, it can strengthen us. Help us to look to and trust God more. It's not like people say about him never giving us more than we can handle. It's more like, we need to realize we need him to help us handle us. We can't forget about him, or think we can do it ourselves. Sometimes it's something that comes out of nowhere, and blindsides us. Sometimes we make bad decisions that lead to bad consequences. Sometimes people even find God through, or even because of, our suffering.

             (Looks at Margaret)

I hope you do. I hope you find some peace through all the pain.

                  MARGARET

Thanks, and I hope my girls grow up to be a teenager like you.

             (LUKE takes proud notice)

DAUGHTER

Thanks. But you can start them on their way by setting an example. Ask Christ into your heart, and let your kids know... And let them know why you did it.

MARGARET

(Slightly embarrassed)

I... I don't know...

MICHAEL

Just ask for a Bible when you get to your room... No, I'll get you one. I'll find one and bring it to you. I'll read the Gospel of Mark with you, if you'd like.

MARGARET

The Gospel of Mark? Why Mark? Why not John?

MICHAEL

Because Mark deals with what we've been talking about... Jesus as a suffering servant...

(All freeze)

PASTOR MESSAGE HERE. ANOTHER QUESTION MAY BE INCORPORATED HERE PER PASTOR'S REQUEST.

GOSPEL OF LUKE SKETCH

(THIRD WEEKEND IN DECEMBER)

The scene is as before, picking up as if MICHAEL has finished speaking to MARGARET about Mark's Gospel.

LUKE

(Somewhat snide)

So. The Gospel of Mark is a good first read for Margaret here … What about me?

MICHAEL

Well, Ummm...

(Gestures for name)

LUKE

Luke. Luke Orderly. Certified Public Accountant.

MICHAEL

Well. Luke. Reading the Bible is a very personal thing. I've read certain scriptures numerous times, and then one day when I read it again...Bam! The Lord hits me with a meaning that had escaped me all those years. Even the different Bible versions may speak to one individual and not another. For instance, I like the English Standard Version, my wife likes the Holman Christian Standard bible, and

my sister gets more out of the New
American Standard bible.

                    LUKE

See! That's just not right.

                    MICHAEL

What? Why?

                    LUKE

Because you need to have all your
ducks in a row... 1-2-3-4-5, 1040,
1040EZ, Schedule C, D, E and F. If
there is no specific order, no logical
progression, and there isn't one way
to do things... well, then...

                    DAUGHTER

There is only one way, Dad. Jesus said
He was the Way. No one gets to the
Father except through Him.

                    LUKE

I'm not talking about what Jesus'
said ... I'm talking about His life. Or
at least the accounts of it. When He
was here on this earth, He was human,
right?

                    MICHAEL

Fully man, and fully God. Yes.

                    LUKE

Then why do we have all these Gospels
that jump around all willy nilly,

and confused like?! Not one gives an orderly account of Jesus' life. Then there's this little problem that they don't agree 100% on the bottom line sometimes. In my line of work, you get fines for that, you know.

MICHAEL

(Snaps his fingers.)

Luke!

LUKE

What?

MICHAEL

(Gesturing like it's obvious)

Luke.

LUKE

(Frustrated as he is right there)

What?

MICHAEL

(Realization)

No! Luke. The Gospel of Luke. You should read it first. It's not necessarily a biography of Jesus' life. But it is a rather orderly account of His life.

LUKE

Oh, please! Luke's Gospel is just a copy of the other Gospels. They all say the same things. Look, repetition is great … if you're advertising a product, and you aren't plagiarizing someone else's work.

MICHAEL

Well… You're right. Luke does write about many of the same events recorded in the other Gospels like: healing the sick, giving sight to the blind, comforting those in need, raising the dead.

LUKE

Wait a minute. The story is that Jesus rose himself from the tomb. He didn't raise anybody else from the dead.

DAUGHTER

(Looking exasperated)

Can you get him a Bible too, when you pick up one for Margaret? Please?

MICHAEL

(Laughs, then to Luke)

She's right, Luke. You do need to read up and study a little. Ever hear of Lazarus?

LUKE

Sure... Lazarus.

DAUGHTER

And why is that name famous, Dad?

LUKE

Lazarus?... Because.... Uh... because by looking at you two, Jesus must have raised him from the dead.

(they nod)

MATT

Don't forget the little girl.

LUKE

(looking around)

Little girl? What little girl?

MATT

(Waves his hand in a no big deal motion.)

Jesus brought a daughter of a temple leader back to life, too. Ordered everyone not to say anything about it.

MICHAEL

Not ordered, requested. And yet, the word did get out. The event is recorded in Mark's Gospel. But, again... That's not really what Luke is concentrating on in his report. In his Gospel.

LUKE

Ok, so I'm no theologian. I'm a CPA. And like I've been saying, I don't go for all that artistic, fancy writing we see in the Bible.

MICHAEL

Which is why I think it would be a
good start for a guy like you. The
Gospel of Luke has a strong emphasis
on historical detail. As well as
showing a great understanding of Jesus
and those around Him. Look, Luke
starts his gospel by pointing out that
lots of people have written accounts
about Jesus, about how He fulfilled
prophecy, performed miracles and the
like... But Luke, has painstakingly
researched and investigated these
accounts... and his Gospel is his final
report. His conclusions.

LUKE

Impossible. How could he do any
intensive research without a
government grant?

MICHAEL

(Smiles)

Well, Luke addresses his Gospel to a
guy named Theophilus, who very well
may have been his benefactor.... But,
that aside... In Luke's day, research
would have run the gamut from scouring
through all sorts of written accounts,
to interviewing eyewitness of the
events in Jesus' life. Luke probably
questioned those people himself.

LUKE

Still, I hear the accusation all the time that Luke's Gospel is just a copy of Mark's Gospel, as well as Matthew's. Nothing's original in it.

MICHAEL

Well, like I said a minute ago, Luke mentions that others had written about Jesus. He doesn't say that he relied on their reports. And, let's face it, you can't have it both ways; you can't complain that Luke has nothing new to offer, and then complain that he believes in and records some events that others also confirm what happened.

ORGANNA

That's like the Yin and the Yang. The real truth is that all religions, all beliefs, lead to God.

MICHAEL

(stares at her for a beat or two)

Ignoring that remark for now... There are some other interesting differences about Luke's account that many people don't realize, though. For instance, Luke wrote in Greek, quite eloquently actually, and his style is such that it indicates he was more interested in reaching Gentiles than Jews. His focus is, more or less, on reality. He says,

"This is what happened, here are the facts, Now, what are you going to do with it?"

LUKE

Do with it? Look, all anyone can do with anything like this is read it, and then decide yes or no, vote it up or down ... That's the way the world is. Black and white.

DAUGHTER

No, Dad. That's the way God is, not the world. If you'd come to church and Sunday school once in a while, you might learn some of these things. Luke wants us to know that the things he writes about Jesus are true... Now, it's up to us to believe and accept Jesus as our Savior—or reject Him, and lose eternal life.

LUKE

(playfully)

And if you're so smart, little girl, prove to me that Luke's account of Jesus is an orderly account of events.

DAUGHTER

Well... There's three major parts to it...

(all freeze.)

PASTOR MESSAGE HERE. ANOTHER QUESTION MAY BE INCORPORATED HERE PER PASTOR'S

REQUEST.

GOSPEL OF JOHN SKETCH

(FOURTH WEEKEND IN DECEMBER)

The scene is as before, picking up as
if DAUGHTER has finished talking about
the Gospel of Luke, and the others
all sort of talking at once. Except
Organna.

ORGANNA

Excuse me! But I am trying to reach my
center here!

LUKE

(After a beat or two where
everyone stares at ORGANNA)

Huh?

ORGANNA

I am trying to go deep into my
transcendental center, in order to
commune with the naturalistic oneness
of all.

(Closes eyes and hums.)

God, I am. Serenity now....

LUKE

(Everyone looks around at
each other, rather amused,
but also confused.)

Again, I ask you. Huh?

ORGANNA

All this talk about Jesus, the Bible,
and prophecy.

(waves it off)

Merely shows that you have not been
lifted to one single enlightened
level yet. Your understanding
substitutes the fact that Jesus was an
enlightened one. That he had reached
full maturity. Unlike all of you.
And me ... to some extent. Jesus had
already lived several lives, thereby
experiencing all of life and what it
has to offer.

MATT

(Looks to MICHAEL)

And now we delve into the wonderful
world of religion, part two! The
Woodstock faith.

MICHAEL

(To MATT)

At least they were The Grateful Dead.
And not the Reincarnated Lives...

(to ORGANNA)

I'm sorry, Miss...?

ORGANNA

Organna. No Miss. No last name. Just
Organna.

DAUGHTER

Oh! Like Jewel... Or... Scooby...

MATT

Or Prince... Or the artist formerly known as Prince, and then known again as Prince...or something like that.

MICHAEL

OK. Look. I apologize if we interfered with your meditations, Organna. But could you please tell me how you know that I or anyone else here is not enlightened?

ORGANNA

Because of the discussions you all have been going on about. All your talk about an antiquated religion.

MICHAEL

Antiquated? You know, the Ten Commandments are older than the New Covenant of Jesus Christ... and the last time I looked, they were still good to go. Can you tell me what it is about them that is outdated?

MARGARET

Here comes the free love argument, I bet.

ORGANNA

Oh, no. There are too many others

issues tied to that. Disease,
paternity, abortion.... No... that...

                    MICHAEL

What then? Which of the Ten
Commandments should we disregard?

                    ORGANNA

The most obvious one is to honor your
mother and father. My father was a
drunken loser. Not worthy of my or
anyone's respect or love.

                    MICHAEL

          (Nods head in understanding)

I understand... My mother raised me
and my four brothers by herself after
my father abandoned us for a life on
skid row...

                    ORGANNA

So, you agree with me...

                    MICHAEL

No, not at all. You see, Organna, the
fifth commandment, honor thy mother
and father is easy for those that
have had loving, caring parents. But
for those of us that have had abusive
parents, or parents that have done,
or maybe continue to do, dishonorable
things... well... for this group...
the challenge is to honor our parents
as far as the relationship will
allow... all the while keeping watch

on our hearts so that we don't repay
them with an evil, for the evil that
they have done to us... We don't want
to prolong a broken relationship that
is ready to be restored. At the same
time, we don't want to allow ourselves
to be in an unhealthy, and unbiblical
relationship with a person who will
only abuse us.

ORGANNA

Might be easy for you...

MICHAEL

I didn't say it was easy.

ORGANNA

Well. Dealing with it as we may, the
truth of it is, in order to reach a
higher plane, the pain inflicted on
us by our parents is just another
experience we must have. We need to
experience all that this life is:
wealth, poverty, murder, sickness...

LUKE

Whoa. Wait a minute... Murder? You
mean I have to go get myself killed?

MATT

Or go kill someone?

ORGANNA

Well, yes sort of.... Once you become
enlightened, however, you will realize

that we should all love one another,
because we are all one. God I am.

                    LUKE

             (mutters)

I guess I'm not ready to be
enlightened.

                  ORGANNA

Let's say you were murdered in a
previous life. You would need to come
back here to murder someone in order
to experience both sides of the issue.
It's these experiences that make us
whole. Of course...

             (uses hands and fingers to
             make the "quote" sign)

... "murder" is an extreme example.

                    LUKE

An extreme example of lunacy. So, you
must be here waiting to see if your
murder victim survives?

                  ORGANNA

No. My significant other was having an
assisted out of body experience... and
the peyote prescription was a little
too high.

                    MATT

Here on this antiquated world, we call
that a drug overdose.

                    LUKE

Or a felony.

ORGANNA

(Obstinate)

My companion's situation has no
bearing on the truth of what we are
discussing here. People who believe in
the Bible are still searching for true
enlightenment.

MICHAEL

I don't know, Organa. I'd argue that
we found it, and those that think they
have to live multiple lives for an
understanding are the ones searching.
Constantly searching.

MARGARET

(to ORGANNA with some
disdain.)

And, Organna... Are you suggesting
that I wanted this cancer? That I
chose to be inflicted with it? That I
needed it to become whole?

ORGANNA

I know at this point in your quest,
it seems odd. But it's because you're
not at a high enough enlightened level
that makes you feel that way. Maybe
in a previous life, you were a doctor
that helped cancer patients, and now
you want to see what it's like to be a
cancer patient.

MARGARET

I think oncologists deal with enough
cancer patients to have a pretty good
idea as to what it's like...

MICHAEL

How about this, Organna? You claim we
come back for multiple lives...

(ORGANNA nods)

Let me ask you two questions: One, how
do we know when we have experienced
every possible scenario in life? Who's
keeping count? And two, why don't
we just make ourselves experience
everything right now... while we're
here.. or better yet, raise yourself
from the grave, just like Jesus
did.... that way we don't have to
waste time with all the growing up and
all.

ORGANNA

There you go again... Do you really
believe all that? What proof do you
have that causes you to believe in
the deity of just one man, Jesus of
Nazareth?

(all freeze.)

PASTOR MESSAGE HERE. ANOTHER QUESTION
MAY BE INCORPORATED IF REQUESTED